# Clarice Bean

## What Planet Are You From?

This book has been printed on paper made from sustainable forest timber.

# Lauren Child

For      Charles      Nick      Andrew      and most especially
Bridget

Thank you
Harriet,
Emma,
Katie, Ruth
and all of the Garrett family

thanks
to my
grandad....
Robert

with love and thanks
to the real life gorgeous morten

ORCHARD BOOKS First published in Great Britain in 2001 by Orchard Books
This edition published in 2009 by The Watts Publishing Group • 10 9 8 7
Copyright © Lauren Child, 2001 and 2009 • The moral rights of the author and illustrator
have been asserted • All rights reserved • A CIP catalogue record for this book is available from the British Library.

ISBN 978 1 40830 005 3 • Printed and bound in China

MIX
Paper from
responsible sources
FSC
www.fsc.org    FSC® C104740

Many thanks to Milo Photography for
the picture of Morten

Orchard Books, an imprint of Hachette Children's Group. Part of The Watts
Publishing Group Limited • Carmelite House, 50 Victoria Embankment
London EC4Y 0DZ • An Hachette UK Company • www.hachette.co.uk
www.hachettechildrens.co.uk

Usually
I rush out of school
like a lunatic.

In school we are learning about the planet of Earth.
Our planet earth is quite small
compared to Jupiter or Saturn, but compared
to the sun Pluto is a peppercorn.

It's hard to think of ourselves living on a planet because it doesn't feel like we are standing on something round.

It's amazing the sea doesn't spill off at the edges, but that's gravity for you.

Gravity is a strange invisible force.

You know it's there because you are not floating about like a jellyfish.

Sometimes I think gravity is a pity.

Mrs Wilberton wants us to do a project called
**The Environment,**
which is nature really.

She has given us little books to write in.

Nature is something I know lots about. We've got lots of it in our garden. There's even nature in the Baldini brothers' garden.

Although you wouldn't think so to look at it, it's mainly dustbins and concrete and a bit of an old car.

Robert Granger lives nearby
and he is always trying to walk home with me.
He says,

Hey, Clarice Bean, **wait for me.**

Luckily,
I
am
a
fast
walker.

When I get home,
	Grandad is buttering
his tie into his sandwich.
He hasn't noticed, he's
	too busy watching a
programme about nature.

Grandad loves nature
	especially when it's Australian.
He likes the idea of living somewhe
where not many people are.
	In Australia you can drive
for maybe squillions of days
without noticing a single
		supermarket, just maybe a
kangaroo, or a wombat.

He says,
I can picture myself sitting in a deckchair
on the top of Uluru,

listening to the cricket.

But I'm just as happy
watching the world go by
under the tree
in Navarino Street.

That's our street.

I am busy thinking about
trees and planets and
# holes
in the sky.

I am sure there is a big hole above our house
because my sister Marcie
uses too much hairspray
and is causing pollution.

spray 'n' hold

No ideas
are coming into my head
for a project.

My mind is a blanket.

So I go upstairs
and read my comics
with the vests and pants
in the airing cupboard.
(Dad says,
If it's **nature**
you are after you should
have a peek in Kurt's bedroom,
it's a regular safari in there.)

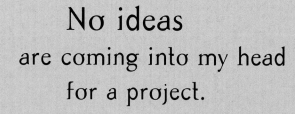

I am reading away when I hear a commotion. It's coming from the kitchen.

So I scriggle down to see what's going on.

What's happened is, my brother Kurt has rushed in and I can see straightaway that he's not normal because he is **running.** (He never runs.) He is flapping the local newspaper about.

Dad says, What on **earth** has got into him?

Cement → our dog

Mum says,

*It's his hormones, they are playing havoc at the moment.*

*Hormones are things which buzz about in your body, making you find your family embarrassing and causing pimples.*

The paper says,

TREE
TO BE
CHOPPED
DOWN IN
NAVARINO
STREET.

It's a really nice tree too
and it is maybe even
at least a hundred years old.

Kurt says,

I won't have any dinner
because I am
too depressed
to chew.

Grandad
switches off
the television,
so of course
we know he's upset.

Dog
Soap

The next day, I am a little bit late for school.
Mrs Wilberton tells me
I have been paired up with
Robert Granger for my project.
She's done that on purpose.
Noah and Betty Moody
are doing a project
about recycling,
which is all about what to do
with your old rubbish,
which is absolutely
not
dropping it
in the
street.
If we even drop one piece
of litter
my mum will go,
*Pick that up at once,*
*you litter bug.*
Sometimes
she runs after people,
waving their rubbish at them.
It's very embarrassing.

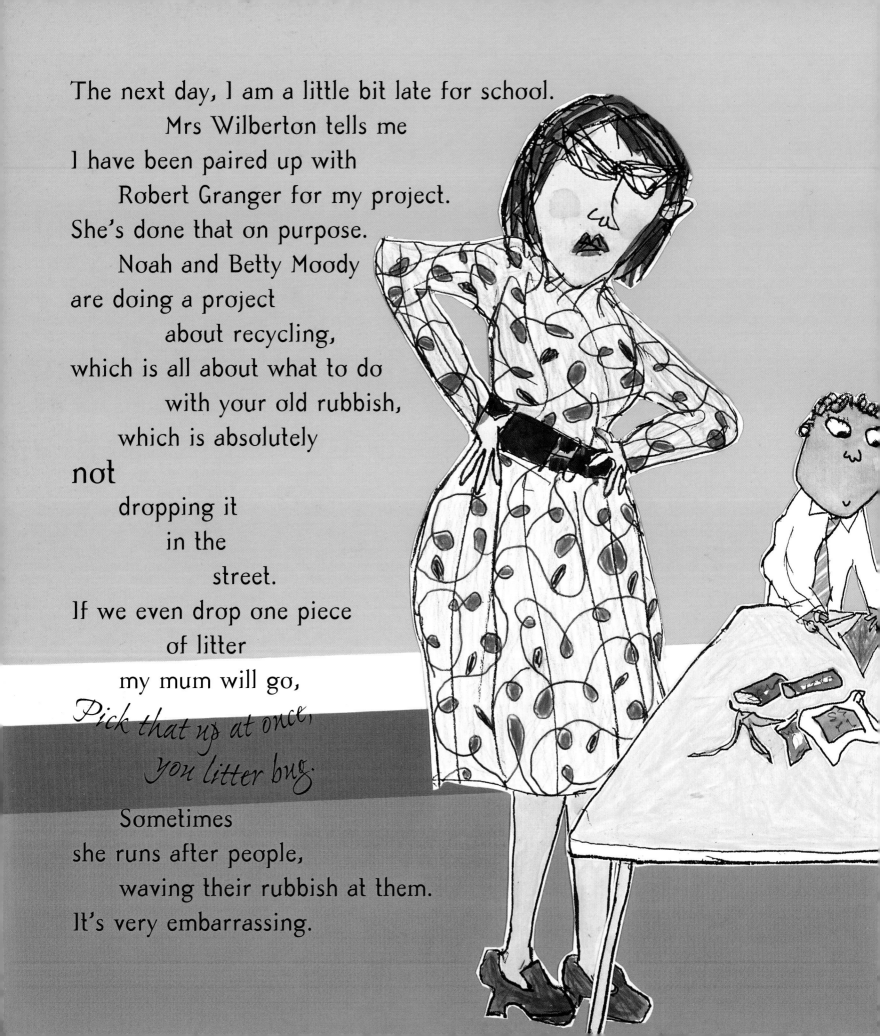

Robert Granger
      is making us do a project on
'Who can walk faster: a snail or a worm?'
      I say,
But that's not important,
                              Mrs Wilberton.

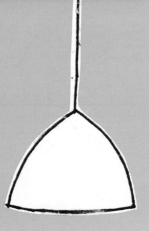

Mrs Wilberton says,
      People who are late
for school don't have
a leg to stand on.

I want to say that's
funny I've got two.
      But I don't
or it would be a trip
to see Mr Pickering
our headmaster.

At least things are exciting at home.

Kurt and his friend Morten are going to camp up the tree. Kurt says he's going to become an eco-warrior. He's got a tent and everything.

Dad says, How are you going to **pitch** a tent up a tree?

Kurt isn't listening.

He says, **We are going to make a plan of action to stop all the destruction.**

Dad mutters, It's a **shame** he doesn't take action over all the destruction going on in his bedroom.

Mum says, *I'm just pleased Kurt is going to do something which involves the word action.*

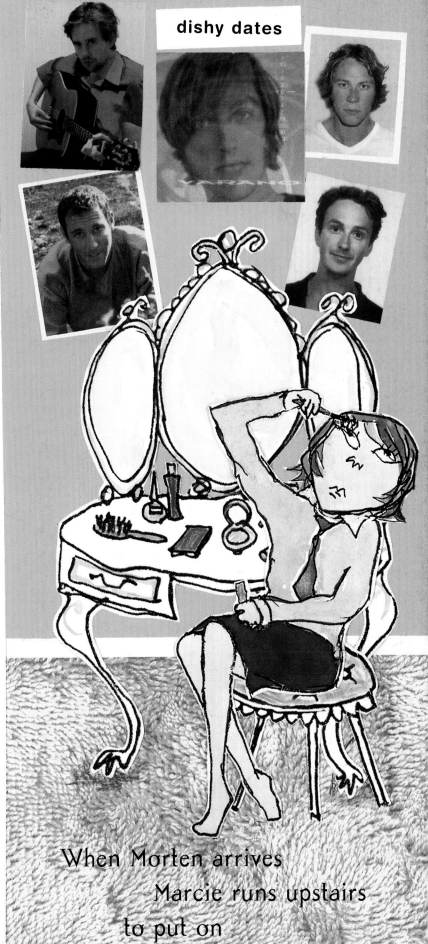

dishy dates

When Morten arrives
Marcie runs upstairs
to put on
MORE make up.

Kurt and Morten have been gone for several hours and people are beginning to worry themselves sick,

   ie Mum.
So when it's eight o'clock we go out to see how they are getting on.

They are sitting outside their tent. Grandad is there with a thermos flask and his friend Bert the Shirt. We don't know why he is called Bert the Shirt, he just always is.

Then Robert Granger comes trotting along.
I just can't get rid of him.

He says,

Why is your brother camping, **Clarice Bean?**
Is he on holiday?

I say,

No one goes on holiday in their own street, nit wit.

They're having a protest.

He says,

They can't be protesting,
they haven't got any signs.

Kurt goes a bit down in the mouth.
Mum tries to cheer him up. She says
she's really proud of Kurt and Morten
and keen on what they are up to.

Marcie's just keen on Morten.

So after school on Wednesday
me and Noah make some posters.
Of course Minal,
my squirty younger brother
wants to join in.

We write, Free the Tree,
because it rhymes really.

Hands Off

Noah is mostly doing the pictures.
Noah is a good drawer.
He can draw anything except
for a camel or a horse.
So don't bother asking him.

Kurt is very pleased
with our posters
and he slightly
smiles even though
Minal has made
a bad spelling
mistake.
And no one can
spell the word
'environment'.

When we have finished
we all go down to the tree.
We leave a note for Dad
because, of course,
he's still working like a maniac.

Free the Tree

Hands Off

When Dad gets home
   he wonders where all the
quiet is coming from,
then he sees our note.

up tree
bring
food

He decides to make us
some spaghetti bolognaise.
(No meat because Kurt won't
eat anyone with four legs or feathers.)

Dad would much rather
cook for a living

I like to cook too.

I do ketchup on toast and in summer salad cream on a tomato.

but he's up to his ears in the wheeling and dealing business and someone's got to bring home the bacon.

Hardly any washing-up is involved.

We are all sitting up the tree eating spaghetti and then suddenly someone nips out and takes our photo.

The next thing we know,
    we are all famous in the local paper.

Hands Off

Of course
    Robert Granger
    gets himself in the picture.

When I get to school I am in BIG trouble.
Mrs Wilberton wants to know why I am late **again**
and where the dickens
is my snail and worm project.

I say,
I've been up till all hours
              saving the planet in our street.

       Mrs Wilberton says,
              I can assure you I will be calling your mother.
    I say,
She can't get to the phone right now Mrs Wilberton,
                                    because she's up a tree.

       Mrs Wilberton says,
       Right, that does it young lady,
we do not tolerate nonsense in this class.

       Robert Granger says,    But it's true **Mrs Wilberton**.

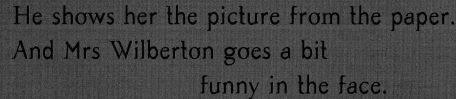

                     He shows her the picture from the paper.
                     And Mrs Wilberton goes a bit
                                    funny in the face.

And
that is
the
absolutely
only time
Robert
Granger
has been
useful,
**ever.**

# My Project

This week I have been being an eco-warrior.

Free the Tree

Being an eco-warrior means you must use recycled toilet paper because toilet paper is made out of trees.

Trees are important
because they are stopping
the earth running
out
of
air.
If we didn't have trees
We would all live in bubbles like space men.

Trees are also like
gynormous
vacuum cleaners
sucking up the
pollution.

There is much more to trees
than twigs and leaves.

And that is why some people
think it is important to sit up a tree
even if it is raining
and you have to be late
for one measly day of school.

Mrs Wilberton does a smile
which is a bit tight at the edges.

But of course she has to say,
Well done Clarice Bean!

The illustrations in this book
are made from all sorts of
RECYCLED THINGS:

magazine clippings,

old photographs,

WRAPPING PAPER,

scraps of fabric

and even bits of newspaper.